American Slavery and
the Fight for Freedom

READ WOKE

SLAVERY AND RECONSTRUCTION

THE STRUGGLE FOR BLACK CIVIL RIGHTS

Elliott Smith
Cicely Lewis, Executive Editor

Lerner Publications ◆ Minneapolis

LETTER FROM CICELY LEWIS

Dear Reader,

Growing up, I learned about Black history only in February. There was a small section in our history textbook about slavery, and then we discussed the Civil Rights Movement. That was it. I always wondered about my ancestors. Did they fight back? How could someone own another human being? What happened between slavery and the Civil Rights Movement?

Cicely Lewis

Then I went to college and took an African American literature class. My whole world opened up as I learned about my history. I started researching and seeking more information. Looking back, I felt like I had been tricked. Why hadn't I learned these things sooner?

As an educator, I want to make sure my students never feel this way. I want you to know:

- Black history didn't begin with slavery.
- Neither Abraham Lincoln nor the Civil Rights Movement ended racism.
- Black people have always fought back.

I want to share the strength, power, *joy*, complexity, and beauty of Black history. This is the gift I hope to give you with this series—but don't stop here. Seek out knowledge wherever you go and question everything.

Yours in solidarity,

—Cicely Lewis, Executive Editor

TABLE OF CONTENTS

Think critically about the photos and illustrations throughout this book. Who is taking the photos or creating the illustrations? What viewpoint do they represent? How does this affect your viewpoint?

These people were once enslaved. Many enslaved people used the Civil War as an opportunity to escape. Once free, they had to build new lives from nothing.

UNEASY FREEDOM

IN THE CIVIL WAR (1861–1865), THE NORTHERN UNION AND THE SOUTHERN CONFEDERACY BATTLED OVER SLAVERY. The years after the South's defeat, called the Reconstruction period (1865–1877), brought freedom to four million formerly enslaved people in the United States. But what did that freedom mean?

After the trauma of slavery, Black people had to build their lives from scratch. Many important facets of modern

Black life were created during Reconstruction. Black colleges were founded. Black churches provided help for the newly free. The first Black men were elected to seats in the US government.

But Black people continued to face hardship. Though the government had promised land and support for the newly free, the promise was not fulfilled. States in the South were slow to recognize the laws that made slavery illegal. Different racist systems ensured that, in many places, Black people's freedom was still limited.

Convict leasing allowed Black people to be arrested on small charges and then forced to perform unpaid labor.

Decades after the end of Reconstruction, Jim Crow laws segregated white and Black people in daily life.

One strategy white people used to prevent Black people's advancement was the passage of so-called Black codes. These were restrictive laws designed to prevent Black people from owning property, voting, using public services, and more.

The Thirteenth Amendment abolished slavery. But it featured a loophole that allowed slavery to continue as punishment for a crime. White people in power created ridiculous crimes and used them to disproportionately arrest free Black men. White law enforcement officers might issue fines knowing that many of those who had been enslaved could not pay them. In those cases, Black people could be convicted and forced to work to repay their debt. The system of convict leasing spread throughout the South. In some cases, free people were forced to work for their former enslavers.

"Enormous populations of African Americans had been returned to a state of slavery," author Douglas A. Blackmon said.

Eventually, the passage of the Fourteenth and Fifteenth Amendments would weaken the Black codes. But their legacy was not forgotten in the South. They would eventually become the basis of laws called Jim Crow that continued to restrict Black people for decades.

"We claim exactly the same rights, privileges and immunities as are enjoyed by white men—we ask nothing more and will be content with nothing less."

—Report from the
Colored Convention of Alabama, 1867

Black women and children near their homes in South Carolina in 1866

CHAPTER 1
WHAT WAS RECONSTRUCTION?

AFTER THE CIVIL WAR, MILLIONS OF RECENTLY FREED PEOPLE NEEDED HELP TO BEGIN THEIR NEW LIVES. They had no resources, jobs, or land. In 1865 the US government ordered that newly free families receive up to 40 acres (16 ha) of land, but the order was soon reversed.

Radical Republicans from the North and conservative Democrats from the South argued about the future of the country. Many from the North wanted to see the South punished for causing the Civil War. Republicans wanted to ensure that free men gained voting rights. Democrats, led by President Andrew Johnson, were open to letting states in the South decide their own laws.

Congress debated about which kinds of help to extend to the newly free. In 1865 they established the Freedmen's Bureau to help formerly enslaved people with housing, food, and other needs. The bureau built hospitals, helped reconnect

A schoolroom created by the Freedmen's Bureau in Richmond, Virginia, in 1866

Black sharecroppers picking cotton in Georgia around 1867

families who had been separated, and established more than one thousand Black schools.

The Fourteenth and Fifteenth Amendments were landmark laws. They gave newly free people rights as American citizens, including the right to vote. But those rights were often ignored by state and local governments, especially in the South. White people used fear, laws, and access to land to keep control of Black people.

REFLECT

How do you think newly free people felt about the abolition of slavery and how to move forward?

Sharecropping was a system where white landowners allowed Black renters to farm land in exchange for a share of the crop. Many Black families grew cotton, tobacco, and rice. But high interest rates and unfair landlords led to Black families becoming indebted to landowners. They were unable to leave until they repaid their debts. Landowners received labor and rental income while their renters struggled. Lacking support and opportunity, many formerly enslaved people were forced into sharecropping and other predatory systems.

COLLEGE HISTORY

Many well-known historically Black colleges and universities (HBCUs) were founded during Reconstruction. Many were founded by Black churches to be independent from the US government. Morehouse College, Fisk University, Howard University, and others sought to educate Black students, who were banned from most other universities. These colleges have a storied legacy and continue to shine as highly ranked schools.

Howard University in Washington, DC, in the 1880s

A state constitutional convention in Richmond, Virginia, in 1868

CHAPTER 2

MAKING GAINS

DESPITE THE MANY OBSTACLES THE NEWLY FREED FACED, THEY BEGAN TO ASSERT THEIR RIGHTS AS AMERICAN CITIZENS. Many Black activists entered politics. In 1867 Black men took part in state constitutional conventions for the first time. These conventions helped to create new state laws after the Civil War. During Reconstruction, more than two thousand Black men held political offices around the country.

Hiram Rhodes Revels of Mississippi became the first Black member of Congress in 1870. Fifteen more Black men were elected to the House and Senate over the next seven years. South Carolina congressional representative Robert Smalls had been enslaved in his early life. He was elected to Congress in 1874.

"It really does reflect what a revolutionary period Reconstruction was," said Gregory Downs, University of California, Davis, history professor. "In a series of a few months, you had people . . . who had been [enslaved] as recently as two or three years before now participating,

Hiram Rhodes Revels

A Black church in Richmond, Virginia, during Reconstruction

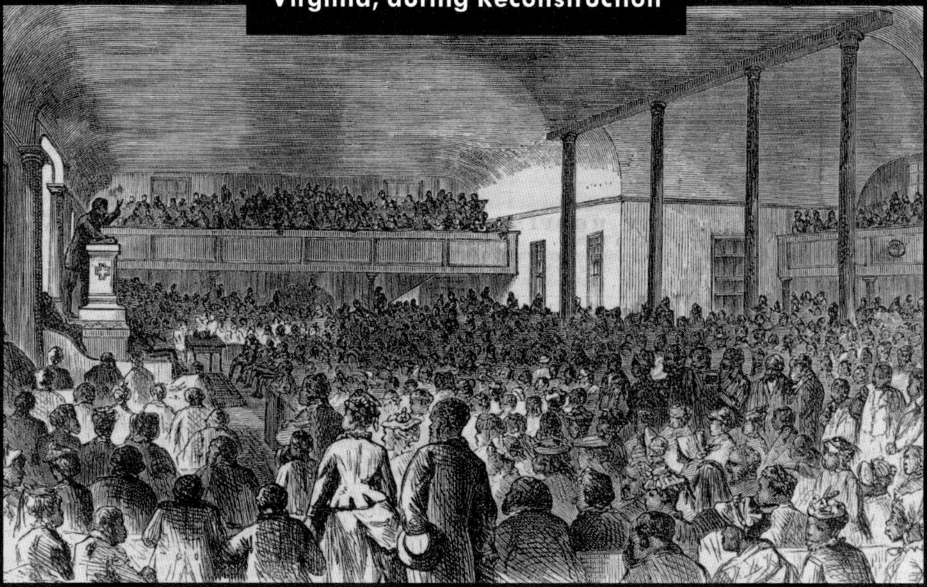

now voting and even being elected to serve to remake the Constitution."

Another important Reconstruction development was the growth of the Black church. Instead of sharing worship with white people, free Black people formed their own churches. Black communities pooled money to buy land and build houses of worship. Churches often served as communities' central gathering spots. They also helped people learn about the politics of their area and to organize into groups to fight for Black interests.

Family was another big part of Reconstruction life. During slavery, enslaved families were often broken up, and relatives were sold to the highest bidder. In the Reconstruction era, newly free Black men and women used churches, local Black papers, and networks of friends to search for lost loved ones. Many families were happily reunited.

RELIGION IN BLACK COMMUNITIES

Enslaved Africans worked to keep their diverse religions and cultural traditions alive in slavery. They performed religious songs and dances. They told traditional stories and performed old rituals. The religions of West Africa, where most enslaved people were from, focused on honoring gods, the natural world, and one's ancestors and elders. Some enslaved Africans were Muslim, worshipping Allah as revealed through his prophet Muhammad.

Many enslavers forced enslaved people to convert to Christianity. They used certain biblical passages to justify slavery or to prove that enslaved people should be obedient. But many enslaved people also found hope in Christianity. Certain passages spoke of oppressed people being liberated by God. It was this form of Christianity that took root in Black churches.

Other communities blended African and Christian traditions. Over time, religions in Black communities became as diverse as the people who practiced them.

A member of the Ku Klux Klan in the late 1800s

CHAPTER 3

PUSHBACK

IN THE FACE OF GROWING BLACK SUCCESS, A WHITE BACKLASH EMERGED. A few years into Reconstruction, white people in the South began creating white-only organizations. These groups, such as the White League, were designed to frighten and intimidate free Black people.

The most notorious of these groups, the Ku Klux Klan, was founded in 1865 in Tennessee. Klan members often attacked under the cover of night or while wearing costumes that hid their faces. Klan members tried to prevent Black people from running for office, voting, or owning land. So-called night riders attacked and even killed Black people in their raids. The Klan faced few consequences for its actions, and the group continued to grow.

As newly free people moved into cities with the hope of finding work, conflicts arose. In 1866 Black communities in Memphis, Tennessee, and New Orleans, Louisiana, fought unfair treatment and were met with violence. Other conflicts sparked in the South throughout Reconstruction.

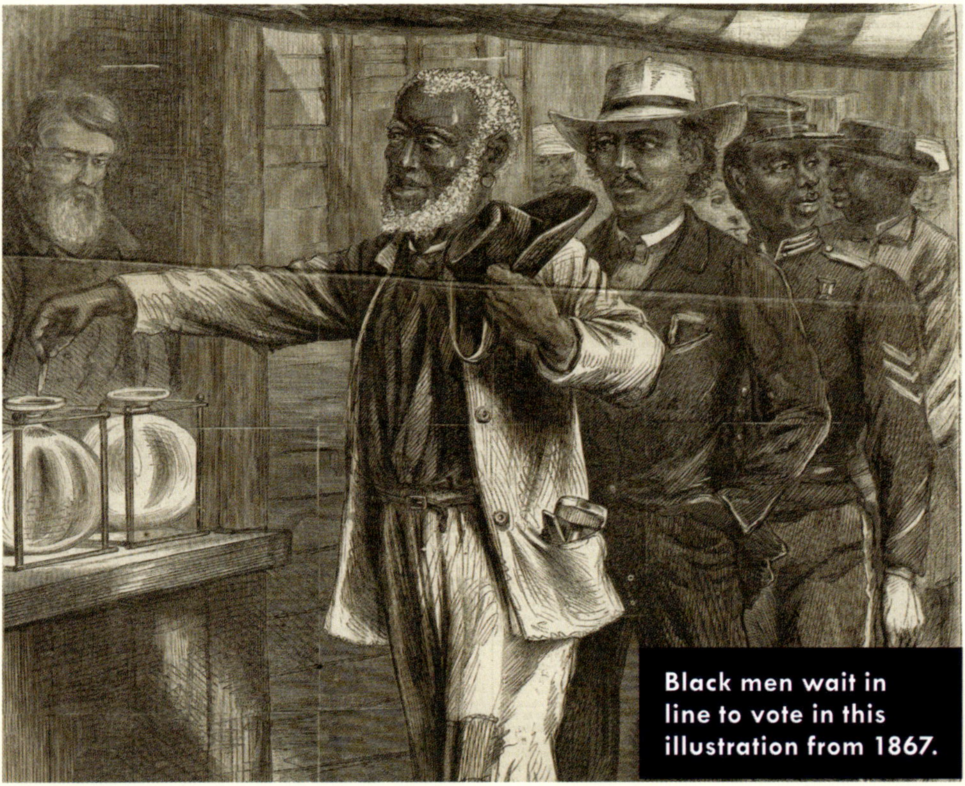

Black men wait in line to vote in this illustration from 1867.

Even in everyday life, Black people encountered harassment and violence. These actions were rarely reported. If they did make it to court, white men were rarely found guilty of any crimes. Many places had laws that prevented Black people from serving on juries, and all-white juries rarely convicted another white person. Thousands of Black people were killed with no justice.

On a national level, two Supreme Court cases stripped away many of the gains the newly free had achieved. The court ruled that the Enforcement Act of 1871, which had banned Ku Klux Klan meetings, was unconstitutional. The court also struck down the Civil Rights Act of 1875. It had prohibited racial discrimination in public places and for services. The rulings weakened the Fourteenth and Fifteenth Amendments, and states began rewriting their constitutions to allow unequal treatment. Then states could suppress the Black vote through measures such as literacy tests and poll taxes.

> "The slave went free; stood a brief moment in the sun; then moved back again toward slavery."
>
> —W. E. B. Du Bois

These illustrations depict the withdrawal of federal troops from the South.

After the end of the Civil War, federal troops remained in the South to help with the reunification of the country. Then the presidential election of 1876 was disputed. Republican Rutherford B. Hayes appeared to be the winner. But Democrats would only agree to confirm Hayes's victory if federal troops left the South. The Compromise of 1877 removed one final layer of protection for newly free Black people.

A café with separate entrances for white and Black people in Durham, North Carolina, in 1940

CHAPTER 4

THE AFTERMATH

THE COMPROMISE OF 1877 MARKED THE END OF THE RECONSTRUCTION ERA. With less federal oversight, governments in the South moved quickly to return to the old ways.

Southern states passed a flurry of so-called separate but equal laws to maintain segregation. These laws created separate schools, parks, transportation, and other facilities for Black and white people. Though the facilities were separate, they were supposed to be equal in quality. But in practice, these laws were simply another form of oppression. The facilities for Black people were often inferior to those for white people. Segregation laws affected Black people for nearly one hundred years.

Black scholars later looked back to evaluate Reconstruction. They had differing opinions about the era's results. Booker T. Washington was disappointed because the reforms of the era didn't give enough people economic freedom. W. E. B. Du Bois

Black soldiers in a segregated recreation room in 1918

Booker T. Washington (*left*) and W. E. B. Du Bois (*right*)

praised the huge expansion of education for Black people but believed the gains made during the period were not enough.

In the face of oppression, Black people showed resistance. They had fought to gain their freedom, and they would fight to keep it.

"This, to me, is the great achievement of Reconstruction," historian Clarence Walker of the University of California, Davis, says. "[It] did not break the Black commitment to racial equality."

REFLECT

Why do you think people in the South were afraid of the political power of Black people?

Dr. Martin Luther King Jr. (*center*) leads the March on Washington for Black civil rights in 1963.

PRIMARY SOURCE VOICES

Scan these QR codes to listen to the actual voices of newly free people as they tell their stories of living through slavery and Reconstruction. As you listen, consider the following: The people in these interviews refer to "slaves." This book uses the term "enslaved people." Why? What is the difference?

As you listen, you can follow along in the transcript linked below each audio clip.

https://www.loc.gov/item/afc1941016_afs05500b/

Harriet Smith, Hempstead, Texas, 1941

https://www.loc.gov/item/afc1984011_afs25750b/

Phoebe Boyd, Dunnsville, Virginia, 1935

https://www.loc.gov/item/afc1941018_afs05091b/

Alice Gaston, Gee's Bend, Alabama, 1941

Who is the woman Alice Gaston refers to as "my missus"? Gaston says the white people treat her "nice."

What do you think these terms mean in the context of slavery?

TAKE ACTION

The Reconstruction era brought about changes that still impact our lives today. Try some of these actions to learn more and make change where you live.

Visit the National Museum of African American History & Culture, or check out its website: https://nmaahc.si.edu.

Explore the *Born in Slavery: Slave Narratives from the Federal Writers' Project, 1936 to 1938* collection at the Library of Congress. This collection contains both first-person accounts of slavery and photos of people who were formerly enslaved. See the collection here: https://www.loc.gov/collections/slave-narratives-from-the-federal-writers-project-1936-to-1938/.

With an adult's help, find out how you can help people in your community to register to vote.

Study the history of an HBCU. Find out when the school was founded, and discover who some of its graduates are.

Learn more about Reconstruction and Black scholars. You can start with the Read Woke Reading List on page 30.

GLOSSARY

Black codes: laws designed to punish or control newly free Black people

Jim Crow: laws designed to segregate and limit the rights of Black people

liberate: to free from bondage or oppression

Reconstruction: the era immediately after the Civil War

scholar: a specialist in a specific area of study

segregation: the legal system of separation of Black and white people

sharecropping: an arrangement in which a landowner allows a tenant to use the land in exchange for a share of the crops produced

unconstitutional: not in agreement with the US Constitution

SOURCE NOTES

7 Douglas A. Blackmon, "Laws to Criminalize Black Life?," *Slavery by Another Name*, PBS video, 2:49, February 12, 2012, https://www.pbs.org/video/slavery-another-name-laws-criminalize-black-life/.

7 Christopher R. Green, *Equal Citizenship, Civil Rights, and the Constitution: The Original Sense of the Privileges or Immunities Clause* (New York: Routledge, 2015), 54.

13–14 Becky Little, "The First Black Man Elected to Congress Was Nearly Blocked from Taking His Seat," History.com, last modified January 27, 2021, https://www.history.com/news/first-black-congressman-hiram-revels.

18 W. E. B. Du Bois, *Black Reconstruction in America 1860–1880* (New York: Simon & Schuster, 1998), 30.

22 "American Experience; Reconstruction: The Second Civil War; Interview with Clarence E. Walker, Historian, University of California, Davis," GBH Archives, accessed March 29, 2021, http://openvault.wgbh.org/catalog/V_3DAC0D0117134D9CB8BFAE03ED053A87.

READ WOKE READING LIST

The African American Odyssey: A Quest for Full Citizenship
https://www.loc.gov/exhibits/african-american-odyssey/reconstruction.html?&loclr=reclnk

America's Story from America's Library: Reconstruction
http://www.americaslibrary.gov/jb/recon/jb_recon_subj.html

Britannica Kids: Booker T. Washington
https://kids.britannica.com/kids/article/Booker-T-Washington/353913

Britannica Kids: Hiram R. Revels
https://kids.britannica.com/kids/article/Hiram-R-Revels/628227

Gates, Henry Louis, Jr., and Tonya Bolden. *Dark Sky Rising: Reconstruction and the Dawn of Jim Crow*. New York: Scholastic, 2019.

Meyers, Walter Dean. *The Glory Field*. New York: Scholastic, 2008.

Miller, Michael. *Exposing Hate: Prejudice, Hatred, and Violence in Action*. Minneapolis: Twenty-First Century Books, 2019.

Nelson, Vaunda Micheaux. *Almost to Freedom*. Minneapolis: Carolrhoda Books, 2003.

INDEX

PHOTO ACKNOWLEDGMENTS

Image credits: Library of Congress, pp. 4, 5, 6, 8, 9, 10, 13, 14, 17, 19, 20, 21, 22; The Miriam and Ira D. Wallach Division of Art, Prints and Photographs: Photography Collection, The New York Public Library, p. 11; VCU Libraries Commons/flickr, p. 12; Everett Collection Historical/ Alamy Stock Photo, p. 16; AP Photo, p. 23.

Cover: Library of Congress; Milano Art/Shutterstock.com (background).

Content consultant: Cleopatra Warren, Ph.D., Secondary History Teacher, Atlanta Public Schools, Atlanta, GA

Lerner Publications Company
An imprint of Lerner Publishing Group, Inc.
241 First Avenue North
Minneapolis, MN 55401 USA

For reading levels and more information, look up this title at www.lernerbooks.com.

Main body text set in Aptifer Sans LT Pro.
Typeface provided by Linotype AG.

Designer: Emily Harris
Lerner team: Martha Kranes

Library of Congress Cataloging-in-Publication Data

Names: Smith, Elliott, 1976– author.
Title: Slavery and Reconstruction : the struggle for Black civil rights / Elliott Smith.
Description: Minneapolis : Lerner Publications, [2022] | Series: American slavery and the fight for freedom (Read Woke Books) | Includes bibliographical references and index. | Audience: Ages 9–14 | Audience: Grades 4–6 | Summary: "With the freeing of four million enslaved people after the Civil War, the Reconstruction period brought new victories and challenges in the fight for Black rights. Learn more about this crucial period in US history"— Provided by publisher.
Identifiers: LCCN 2021007288 (print) | LCCN 2021007289 (ebook) | ISBN 9781728439105 (library binding) | ISBN 9781728444314 (ebook)
Subjects: LCSH: African Americans—History—1863–1877—Juvenile literature. | Reconstruction (U.S. history, 1865–1877)—Juvenile literature. | African Americans—Civil rights—Southern States—History—19th century—Juvenile literature. | African Americans—Southern States—Social conditions—19th century—Juvenile literature. | Southern States—Race relations—Juvenile literature.
Classification: LCC E185.2 .S65 2022 (print) | LCC E185.2 (ebook) | DDC 323.1196/07309034—dc23

LC record available at https://lccn.loc.gov/2021007288
LC ebook record available at https://lccn.loc.gov/2021007289

Manufactured in the United States of America
1-49787-49659-7/2/2021